For Beatrice

First published in Canada by
Stoddart Publishing Co. Limited
34 Lesmill Road
Toronto, Canada
M3B 2T6

Published in Great Britain by
Simon & Schuster
West Garden Place
Kendal Street
London W2 2AQ
United Kingdom

CANADIAN CATALOGUING IN PUBLICATION DATA

York, Sarah, Duchess of, 1959-
Budgie, The Little Helicopter

ISBN 0-7737-2351-X

I. Richardson, John, 1955-   II. Title

PZ7.Y67Bu 1989   j823′.914   C89-094189-0

Typeset in Stempel Schneidler by Pastiche, London
Printed in Great Britain by Cambus Litho Ltd, East Kilbride
Bound by MacLehose & Partners Ltd, Portsmouth

~ BUDGIE ~
The Little Helicopter

H.R.H. The Duchess of York
Illustrated by John Richardson

Stoddart

It was a hot, hot day. Budgie, the helicopter, was bored. He looked around the huge hangar but nothing stirred. Oliver, the owl, was fast asleep and even Fergus, the cat, didn't notice the mouse in front of his nose. Budgie turned on his radio but nothing was happening.

Every now and then he cooled himself with a whirr of his rotors. 'Same old faces,' he thought, as he looked around. 'I wish something exciting would happen.' Budgie always longed for a bit of adventure.

Yesterday Budgie spent the whole day delivering crate
after crate of clawing lobsters from Mulhearn-on-Sea.
'I may be the littlest helicopter,' he sighed to himself, 'but
I wish I wasn't always given the nasty, little jobs to do.'

Yesterday Budgie spent the whole day delivering crate
after crate of clawing lobsters from Mulhearn-on-Sea.
'I may be the littlest helicopter,' he sighed to himself, 'but
I wish I wasn't always given the nasty, little jobs to do.'

Every now and then he cooled himself with a whirr of his rotors. 'Same old faces,' he thought, as he looked around. 'I wish something exciting would happen.' Budgie always longed for a bit of adventure.

How Lionel, the Lynx, laughed when Budgie was forced to have a thorough wash and polish afterwards, because he smelled so fishy. There was nothing Budgie disliked more than a good scrub in the helicopter wash.

Clatter, clatter, clatter, blatter, blatter, clatter.
Budgie looked up and saw Lionel.
'Hurumph!' Lionel cleared his throat. 'Hurumph! Um, this is Budgie,'
he said to a small plane who sparkled and shone.

'He's not usually so clean. Must have been forced to wash.'
Budgie blushed red to the roots of his rotors.
'I'm Pippa,' said the plane. 'I'm new.'
'Hello,' smiled Budgie.

Bang! Bang! Bang! went the bird scarer. Everyone jumped.
'That's for me. It's my first flight today,' said Pippa.
'Can I come?' said Budgie. 'It looks as though there might be a

thunderstorm and I can warn you if there's any danger of lightning.'

'Oh, thank you,' said Pippa. 'Let's go.'

'It's all right for you,' groaned Lionel. 'Some of us have real work to do.'

Pippa soared. She looped the loop. *Wheeee.* Flew on her side. *Brrrr.*

Then swooped. *Eoww.* 'Hurrah, hurrah,' shouted Budgie. 'Well done, Pippa!'

Just then there was a loud noise. *Whoop, whoop, whoop*
it went. *Whoop, whoop, whoop.*
'That's the alarm,' said Budgie.
'Control calling Lionel. Control calling Lionel.

Lionel come in please. Emergency, Lionel. Over.'
Budgie clicked on his radio. *Whrrr.* 'Budgie to Control,
Budgie to Control. Lionel's out on a job and won't be
back for hours. Can we help? Over!'

'Control to Budgie. You and Pippa are much too light and small.
We need Lionel's help. There's a storm brewing.'
Budgie looked at Pippa. 'Too small,' he said. 'Who says we're too
small? Too small for what?'
So Budgie listened to his radio to find out what had happened. Rose
Wright, on her way home from school in Stanton, was stopped by
some men in a car and bundled inside. Now the kidnappers wanted a
huge ransom from her parents. Just as he was noting the details of the
getaway car, Budgie's radio went dead. The sky grew very dark. The
two friends had the same thought at once.
'Come on. Let's go.'
Budgie felt the first drops of rain and heard the thunder. As he watched
the lightning approach, he couldn't help feeling frightened.

Buffeted and blown, Budgie and Pippa arrived at Stanton. They spotted the school as the rain died away. They didn't know which road the car had taken, so they flew in ever widening circles, keeping fairly low. Then Pippa spied a big, black car in the distance. 'Quick,' she said. 'Let's follow them.'

They followed the car for some time. Eventually it turned along a country lane and headed towards an old barn. When the car stopped, Budgie and Pippa flew straight past pretending that nothing was wrong.

'You keep watch, and I'll go for help,' said Pippa. Silently she sped off.

All alone, Budgie flew towards the barn. He turned off his engine
and landed noiselessly. 'Only a light and small helicopter could land
between these trees,' he thought proudly. As he watched and
waited for help to arrive, it began to get dark.

Bang! Crash! There was a loud noise from the barn. Budgie looked up and heard a shout. 'Get after her.'

'Over here, Rose!' Budgie shouted. 'Look out, behind you. Quick, jump up!'
As quick as a wink Rose was on board and Budgie burst into life.

But just as Budgie lifted off the ground the man grabbed one of his skids and hung on.

'This is my chance,' thought Budgie. 'I'll keep him dangling until the
police arrive and arrest him. He can't escape.'

Minutes later Budgie heard a screech of brakes. The police had arrived and he heard a familiar clatter. It was Lionel barking orders. The second kidnapper made a run for it.

'You won't get far,' shouted Budgie.
 Then he carefully positioned himself over the roof of the barn.
'Here we go,' he said as he shook his skids.

'Aaargh!' Crash! Bang! Splat!

Budgie landed gently and Rose jumped out. Her parents were waiting, happy and relieved that she was safe, and Rose ran towards them. Lionel looked on, smiling.

'Brave Budgie saved me,' cried Rose.
Budgie smiled. 'What an exciting day it's been, after all,' he sighed,
as he started for home.

Back at the hangar, Budgie received a hero's welcome.
'Bravo Budgie,' said Lionel.
'I couldn't have done it without Pippa,' said Budgie. 'We make a good team.'

'You'd better come with me,' said Pippa mysteriously. 'Now you're
a hero, you'll have to be cleaned up.'
'Oh no,' moaned Budgie. 'It's nice being made a fuss of...

...but I hate having a bath!'